THE
CREAKING
DEATH

ALSO BY DAVID RALPH WILLIAMS

GHOST STORIES

Olde Tudor
By a lantern's light
Dead Men's Eyes

THE CREAKING DEATH

A Ghost Story

David Ralph Williams

LOXDALE PUBLISHING HOUSE

DAVID RALPH WILLIAMS

This edition 2020 by
LOXDALE PUBLISHING HOUSE
Copyright © David Ralph Williams 2003

Cover painting 'The Gypsea' By Ralph Williams

Thanks to Cathy

I would like to thank you the reader for choosing
this little book amongst the multitudes of other titles
waiting to be discovered. I am forever thankful.

THE CREAKING DEATH

THE CREAKING DEATH

And some in dreams assured were,
Of the Spirit that plagued us so,
Nine fathom deep he had followed us,
From the land of mist and snow.
The Rime of the Ancient Mariner (text
of 1834) by Samuel Taylor (II.31-32)

1

Riding the waves, carried by the wind, the vessel Gypsea with its sails inflated, cut a course towards danger. Many voyages had the Gypsea braved and as its name implied, she almost never remained in one place for too long. The Gypsea was a pirate ship and carried its captain, (the legendary Balthazar Blyberg) and his crew, to far off shores returning lighter for men but leaden with treasures obtained during its plunders.

Captain Balthazar Blyberg, a notorious pirate of vicious disposition, was as feared as any pirate past or present could ever be. Blyberg's marauding became the subject of legends carried coast to coast; some describing him romantically as a sort of highwayman of the sea, whilst others accurately portrayed him as the villain he was. From all the stories and legends one thing prevailed, Blyberg was ruthless and above all should never be crossed.

Captain Blyberg, was barely fully-grown at the time he acquired his ship from the Spanish merchant fleet, some say single-handedly. He filled it with freebooting rogues like himself, gaining their service and respect. All Blyberg's crew were proud to sail under 'Old Roger' the bone and black pennant that told all who would challenge them that the Gypsea took no prisoners.

As a symbol of his total authority over the Gypsea and its crew, Blyberg had carved an impressive figurehead caricature of himself out of cedar wood.

The figurehead graced the bow of the ship and resembled Blyberg in every detail; his black curling locks, wild beard, and dark piercing eyes. He had painted the figurehead himself and it sported the likeness of his own distinctive clothing. Matching Blyberg's own ego, it was an altogether towering garish edifice, almost a deity watching over the ship.

Blyberg and the Gypsea had crossed the seas for many a decade, with its figurehead thrust out to challenge nature's mightiest element. Sometimes during a drinking binge following a successful plunder, the captain could be seen climbing the bowsprit and shouting,

"Even the sea is afraid of me!" over and over, and sometimes during a hellish storm.

After many a year Blyberg grew older, surviving his many battles whilst his crew succumbed to sword and musket and were replaced by men half the age of the old sea dog himself. Captain

Blyberg, like the paint on his figure-head, began to fade and flake. Many of the crew, and in particular, Stobie Shipman, the Captain's old Coxswain, (once in charge of the small cockboat that rowed him to and from the ship), had begun challenging Blyberg's authority. Shipman sought to replace him one day so he could take over as Captain of the Gypsea.

On one occasion, Blyberg ordered Shipman to be keel hauled and the crew reluctantly obeyed. A rope was rigged from yardarm to yardarm passing under the bottom of the ship, and the unfortunate Shipman was tied to it with iron weights attached to his legs. He was hoisted up to one yardarm and then dropped suddenly into the sea, hauled underneath the ship, and finally hoisted up to the opposite yardarm. Shipman almost drowned and never forgot his punishment; swearing revenge to any who listened to him during his regular binges of rum.

From that day on, Captain Blyberg watched his back. Shipman stole more and more respect away from him and after a spate of disastrous exploits he saw Shipman proclaim himself to be the new Captain of the Gypsea, and during one swarthy and uneasy night at sea, mutiny erupted.

2

"Get back! Back I says, you motley gull-brained fools!" roared Blyberg whilst simultaneously shooting his musket into a crowd of his mutinous crew, which had gathered at the door of his cabin. Blyberg lunged forward into the cloud of gunpowder and swung the door of his cabin shut.

Trapped inside the cabin, he remained undefeated. There was only one way in and he had the door covered.

Captain Blyberg knew it was only a matter of time before he succumbed to the might of his crew's rebellion and he drank great mouthfuls of port from his own fine collection, whilst reloading his musket.

So far he had dispatched six of his crew and he was determined to take as many as he could down with him. Blyberg had been clever; anticipating a mutinous outbreak he had poisoned all but three scuttlebutts containing the crews drinking water. He had then dragged the untainted casks into his cabin along with a week's supply of food. Some of the crew were already sick from the poisoned water but the healthy men were more determined than ever to end Blyberg's command. With Stobie Shipman to lead them, they set about a terrible plan.

Shipman went down below decks to the galley and took the smoking lamp off its hook. The smoking lamp was a safety measure, kept down below for the convenience of the tobacco loving crew and also to keep the hazard of fire away from highly combustible wood-work and gunpowder. He carried the lamp back up on deck; it was heavy and full with burning oil. Shipman almost slipped on the sea sprayed deck planks as he made his way quietly back to the door of Captain Blyberg's cabin. A ser-ies of gestures conveyed a message from Shipman to another crewmember who understood what Shipman intended to do with the lamp. The crewman kicked the cabin door inward but sustained the full force of two musket balls fired from Blyberg's weapon.

"Heargh! You think you can outsmart old Blyberg with a trick like that do you? Well I'll show you, I'll show all of you," thundered Blyberg. Shipman used his chance and pitched the smoking lamp through the unguarded doorway. The lamp shattered on the wooden floor and its blazing stream spread to every corner of the cabin. Blyberg leapt on top of the heavy wooden dining table that stood in the centre of the room. The flames licked the legs of the table and he knew he had seconds to escape this growing inferno. Tossing his spent musket to the floor, Blyberg unsheathed a slim but sharp sword from his belt and defying his age, leapt off the table and out of the cabin door into the mutinous mob that waited outside.

Captain Blyberg fought like a lion. Those men who did not feel the cold steel of his willing blade were trampled under-foot, or tossed aside. Many men were preoccupied with dowsing the blaze inside the cabin before the whole ship succumbed. Blyberg only sought out one man, his rival on the ship and instigator of this enmity.

Shipman was waiting for him at the bow of the ship. He was worried. He thought the captain would have been shark bait by now. Instead, he seemed mightier than ever, growing younger with each and every kill. Blyberg dispatched the last of the crew that came to challenge him and turned on the cowering survivors.

"I am stronger than you all together! You cannot kill me, I am as constant as the mountains and the stars that guide us. I am indestructible!" were his jubilant cries. One by one the crew members dropped their weapons and pledged loyalty to their captain.

"Do you think I wants you all now? I should split the whole lot of you open, and feed you to the gulls!" spat a furious Blyberg.

"I-i-it were all his doing skipper. He forced us to go against you he did," stammered a crewman whilst pointing out towards the bow. Blyberg turned and saw Stobie Shipman inching away along the bowsprit that extended out from the bow of the ship to joust with the waves. Blyberg came running, his black eyes like his beard were wild, his angered face shone like crimson coral, and he roared.

Captain Blyberg's roar, and the terrified scream of Stobie Shipman were drowned out by the tumultuous splintering and smashing noise of the Gypsea as she hit the rocks. During the battles, nobody had been at the helm, and the Gypsea was left to cruise off course, wandering ever so dangerously close to the jagged toothed outcrop of rocks a mile or so out from Gull Cove.

These rocks had taken many a ship down over the years which in turn resulted in the construction of Gull Tower, a lighthouse perched high above the cove on the cliff top. However nobody saw its signal through the thick torrents of smoke and sparks that engulfed the smouldering ship.

Everyone was thrown off their feet when she struck. Men like rag dolls tossed about the deck. Stobie Shipman was cast onto the rigging at the bow and was caught like a fly in a vast web. Captain Blyberg was first sent sliding down the bowsprit and then cast back to smash against his figurehead that he somehow managed to hold onto. The Gypsea was sinking fast. A few men dived overboard for fear of being sucked down with her as she continued to flounder. Others were trapped as the main mast toppled down pinning the smashed bodies of crewmen to the deck and ensuring a watery grave for all who lay under.

Stobie Shipman climbed down from the rigging and onto the bowsprit. He unsheathed a hefty dagger and clasped it between his teeth as he shuffled himself along towards the captain. Blyberg was having difficulty holding onto his figurehead and had lost his sword when he had been catapulted forward. Stobie seized his chance and ran his dagger through Blyberg pinning him to the figurehead. The captain moaned in agony as he hopelessly tried to remove the restraining blade; it had gone straight through his side, cutting into a rib or two.

The entire ship tilted backwards elevating the bow and Blyberg towards the stars. Shipman dived off the bowsprit and into the sea. He frantically swam with all his strength to escape the pull of the submerging ship which threatened to suck him into its whirlpool. It almost seemed to grip his ankles, but gradually Shipman managed to escape the pull and continued to swim until his thumping heart warned him to rest. He bobbed upon the waves and cast a glance back towards the sinking ship. The half-moon cast its pale lustre upon the sea and illuminated what remained of The Gypsea. Only the bow of the ship was visible now and Shipman could see the wriggling form of Blyberg, still firmly attached to his figurehead effigy.

"I curse you Shipman. The Gypsea curse you. I'll get you for this I swear, hear my words hear—". Captain Blyberg's dying rants were silenced by a hungry sea. Soon all Shipman could see of the captain was his mop of black curls sitting on the water's surface like a great hairy spider and soon even that was devoured.

3

D own and down sank Blyberg into the murky depths. Weak shafts of moonlight filtered through the surface of the water and were the only comfort on his long way down, as he held onto his breath for an amazing length of time. The pressures of the water crushed his body, but still he lived and remained cursing and hating amongst the crabs and the seaweed. The moonlight could not reach the seabed, but that didn't matter. Blyberg couldn't see anything since his eyes had ruptured. Soon the captain's powerful will alone was not enough to keep him alive. His spirit ebbed away from him as the sea came flooding in, and in Blyberg's last dying moments he felt an embrace, as hard and cold as the sea itself.

Shipman began to swim. It was dark and the sea was cold; icy cold. He believed he would die as well, and sinking to the seabed where his and Blyberg's spirit would battle it out once more, amidst the skeleton crew of a thousand wrecked ships. He was glad to see a large portion of the Gypsea's hull come floating by and swam to it, hauling himself on top. The raft-like lifeboat carried the unconscious sole survivor of the Gypsea towards a flickering light on the horizon; the light which emanated from the lighthouse at Gull Cove.

Old Sam Finn climbed over the ragged rocks below the cliff top on which stood Gull Tower, the lighthouse for which he was the keeper. It was near dawn and the darkness was starting to lift and be replaced by the morning sea mists that rolled on shore to becloud Sam's path. With his lantern held out in front, Old Sam found the entrance to the cavern and clambered inside. The cavern, a natural burrow forged and smoothed by the ocean's fingers was as familiar to Sam as was his cottage that adjoined Gull Tower, his home for a decade or more.

Sam shuffled along the dark passageway of the cavern and rested his lantern down on top of a large pile of boulders at the far end. Heaving himself to the top of the pile Old Sam rested for a moment; he was getting too old for this but he knew this was the safest place to hide his riches. Sam lifted his lantern above his head and found the entrance to the upper chamber, a fissure in the roof that he clambered through.

The upper chamber was darker and had a distinctive sound all of its own. The walls and ceiling were a writhing mass of black spiders. A single spider alone produces virtually no sound, but a billion animals teeming down the walls attracted to a lantern's light is a singularly unpleasant sound. Sam found his prize. An enormous trunk that a decade since he had been able to push through the cavern fissure, but now his ageing body could hardly drag it. Sam opened the trunk and held his lantern inside. The trunk was loaded with bars of gold, trinkets, and heaps of silver coins. Sam filled a small chest he had carried with him on his belt full of coins and hurriedly made his way back across the floor down to the cavern below. The spiders had already started to bite.

Old Sam was back on the rocks now and he turned up the lantern's wick to see through the thickening sea frets. Suddenly he went head over heels, dropping his lantern which smashed on the rocks below. Even though Sam knew his path across the rocks as good as he knew the back of his own fist, he had somehow managed to trip over something that was lying in his path.

He rubbed his grazed elbow and looked down to see what was the cause of his mishap. Lying face up on the rocks was a man. Sam studied the sea washed figure closely. His clothes were all torn, and he wore only one sandal. He had a red scarf tied to his head that partly covered his unruly mop of yellow hair, and his face was littered with the scars of old wounds. Assuming the man was dead, Sam knelt beside him and rummaged through his pockets, which apart from a broken clay pipe were empty.

He got back on his feet and was about to kick the man off the rocks into a watery tomb but stopped himself after the man let out a weary moan. Sam dragged the man to a sitting position and immediately he coughed and spewed forth great mouthfuls of seawater. Delirious, the man raved about the sea swallowing him up. It was Stobie Shipman, his life raft from the hull of the Gypsea had brought him to Gull Cove where he had been tossed onto the rocks during a sea storm. Sam dragged Shipman off the rocks and helped him back to his cottage where the exhausted Shipman was given time to recover on a chair in front of a well-stoked fire.

4

Shipman slept all day on Sam Finn's chair and at nine o'clock in the evening he began to wake up. At first he merely opened his eyes to take in his new surroundings. He was in a small yet cosy room, which was simply furnished. Apart from the chair he was slumped on, there were only two other seats; a small stool near a curtained window, and a rocking chair that was occupied by a snoozing Sam Finn. The walls of the house were whitewashed stone and a couple of them held some basic shelving upon which were placed various items of necessity such as candles and soap. A functional house he thought.

Shipman observed his slumbering rescuer. Sam Finn had the look of an old weather beaten sailor with sun-reddened complexion, a stark contrast to his bleached white hair and beard. He wore a grey broad brimmed floppy hat with a matching long woollen overcoat secured with a rope belt. The old man was poor thought Shipman for he could see nothing in the way of luxurious knick-knacks or embellishment. There was something however that caught Shipman's eye. On top of a sturdy dining table was a small iron chest, which he scrutinised for many a minute.

"Oh, decided to join the land of the living have we!" shouted a merry Sam Finn seeing Shipman was awake and he climbed out of his rocking chair and made his way over to where the pirate was lying.

"Got a name have we?" he enquired

whilst stuffing tobacco into his favourite pipe.

"Aye I have that, but who the hell are you?" replied Shipman now sitting up.

"Who the hell am I? Well I be your saviour see. Pulled you off rocks and brought you to me house I did! That's who I be," answered Sam now lighting his pipe from a nearby candle.

"You not even thanked me, aye, an me risking life and limb," continued Sam.

"Me name be Shipman, Stobie Shipman, and I do thank you if t'was you that pulled me to safety from the devil's own ocean."

"It was. Are you hungry?" asked Sam, now moving towards a door on the far wall.

"No, not hungry. Thirsty though," replied Shipman.

"I bet, it be all the salt water you swallowed. I'll fetch you a drink," said Sam and he disappeared through the door.

Shipman got to his feet and stretched

his arms. He felt rough but nothing out of the ordinary. It wasn't the first time he had found himself shipwrecked. In fact, it was Captain Blyberg who once rescued him from a botched attempt of piracy and subsequently recruited his services on the Gypsea. He cast his mind back to the mutiny and the disaster that followed. Nothing about it had turned out as he'd wanted. He had lost the ship and all its spoils to the murky depths of the sea bed. Shipman desperately wanted something to counterbalance this misfortune, and he moved over to the table to examine the iron chest. It was heavy and when shook it rattled. A pirate with Shipman's experience knew the sound of silver when shaken, and by the weight of the chest he calculated it contained a tidy sum. The old codger must have all his worldly savings in this chest he thought as he turned it over and over in his hands. The iron chest was locked and Shipman placed it back onto the table in time for the re-emergence of Old Sam who was now carrying two steaming mugs of broth.

"Get this down you," said Sam as he handed over a mug of nourishment. Shipman was more interested in the brown bottle he could see poking out from one of Sam's oversized coat pockets.

"Oh, you wants a sip of me rum, do you?"

"Aye if I may, it was a rough night." Shipman joked and he gratefully took the bottle of rum off Sam and took many a swig.

"Steady mate, it's good stuff see," said Sam worried that this stranger would guzzle the lot.

"I need to wet me whistle too mind; I have a night's work ahead."

"Work? What work?" enquired Shipman,

"Jesus to Betsy! Where do you think you are lad? This is a lighthouse, and I be its keeper, Sam Finn, but me friends calls me Sammy see."

Shipman wiped his wet lips on the back of his hand and handed the rum bottle back to Sam.

"Pleased to meet you Sam, and thanks for the drop of rum."

"Aye, it's a good-un all right, I be saving it for a long time see."

Old Sam took up a candle from one of the shelves and lit it using a long wooden taper that he poked into the fire.

"Would you like to come up top of Gull Tower lad? I have to light her."

Sam opened the heavy door which formed a link between the cottage and the lighthouse.

"Aye, never been up a lighthouse before."

Shipman caught sight of Sam's ring of keys that jingled from his belt and guessed that one of them would surely open the iron chest on the table.

The two men entered Gull Tower and Sam used his candle to light a couple of oil lamps that hung off a hook at the foot of a huge, black iron, spiral staircase.

"We needs these see, it's dark up here and I wouldn't want you to fall," chuckled Sam as he gave a lamp to Shipman.

They both ascended the staircase with Sam leading the way. Each and every footfall rang out and reverberated its ferric tones throughout the entire cavity of the tower. Shipman, following Sam close behind, never took his gaze off Sam's ring of keys. Now a slave to his pirate instincts he began to plan how to get his hands on those keys, even if it meant disposing of Old Sam. He imagined taking out his dagger and cutting Sam's throat as he climbed the stairs. Alas, his dagger was lost to the depths of the sea along with Captain Blyberg whose body it had impaled to the Gypsea's figurehead.

5

The iron staircase ended and met with a similarly fashioned heavy door. The door was locked and Sam unhooked his key ring and used one of the keys to open it.

"Have to keep it locked see, what with all the oil. Tis dangerous it is," explained Sam and he led the way to the beacon itself. Sam began about his business of lighting it and did so in such a way that spoke to Shipman of years of service. The beacon consisted of a circular wick housed in a glass chimney that was fed by fish oil. Sam used his portable lamp to light the wick which flooded the tower top with a clear clean bright light.

"Used to be a coal burning fire, but town mayor bought in this here new Swiss invention, good eh?" smiled Sam proud of his beacon. "I call's her, lady 'o the night!" Shipman watched the keeper as he walked over to a protective rail that encircled the entire top of the tower. Sam produced a brass telescope from out of an inside coat pocket and used it to scan the horizon. The moon was full and round and cast a twin onto a smooth, black sea.

"Sea is calm tonight," he observed. "Ships won't be needing me and this old lady's light to protect them. No, not tonight." Shipman merely listened; his eyes big and round, like an owl waiting to pounce.

"Merchant's ship was it, that you lost?" asked Sam.

"Aye, I was Helmsman," lied Shipman.

"Not much of a Helmsman I'd say,

sailing too near to Gull Cove, and breaking up on the rocks. Not even a smidgen of fog to be seen either," teased Sam. "Don't even look like much of a merchant either."

Shipman narrowed his wide eyes and became irritated with Sam's subtle inquisition.

"By your clothes and manner, I'd say you looked more like a pirate!" came Sam's abrupt and surprising remark. Shipman knew the penalty for being a pirate and couldn't take the risk of being caught on the mainland.

"Aye, now comes to think of it, you do look like a pirate lad, and I've seen many I have!" Instinctively, Shipman lunged at Sam grabbing the front of his coat in a threatening manner.

"Well I am a pirate see, I killed me captain and I sunk me ship, and I almost drowned with nothing to show for me troubles bar a belly full of sea water! Now I've found you see, and I wants what you got!" he bellowed.

"I aint got nothing you would want, I am a poor old man," spluttered a now fearful Sam. With a sudden yank Shipman got the ring of keys off Sam's belt and chose the biggest and heaviest key to threaten him with.

"Tell me which key opens the chest, and I might just strangle you instead of splitting you open with this!" he threatened.

"D–don't you do anything hasty. We be brothers you and me; I was a pirate too. Robbed the king's own fleet! That's how I recognised you, a pirate always knows a pirate see."

"Shut yer face you old slyboots. Tell me which key opens the chest," demanded Shipman who now saw Sam in a new light. There was something of the pirate about him.

"I–I can't remember which one exactly," lied Sam. Shipman began to beat the old man with the heavy key, ferociously smashing it and driving it deep into his frail skull until it popped and cracked. Sam lay at Shipman's feet; his head was bloodied and swollen.

"W–wait, d–don't kill me! I'll tell you which key opens me chest," whimpered a broken Sam. It took Shipman only minutes to drag Sam all the way down the iron staircase and back into the cottage.

Sam was half slumped across the heavy table and was slowly sorting through the bunch of sticky keys that were coated in his own blood. He held out a stubby brass key which Shipman snatched and proceeded to unlock the chest. His face lit up with pleasure at the contents. After a brief examination of the heap of silver coins Shipman returned his attention to Sam who was now barely conscious and bleeding pro-fusely from his ears.

"Where's the rest? You being a pir-ate must have more than this squirreled away some place," he boomed. Shipman grasped the heavy key once more and forced Sam to look at him.

"I won't ask you again," he said.

6

Stobie Shipman was back on the same rocks where he had been washed ashore the previous night. He had forced Sam to tell him all about the hidden treasure in the cavern below Gull Tower. The treasure was the accumulation of many of the old Sea Rover's exploits and its total value was apparently beyond calculation. Like many a pirate, Sam merely sat on his fortune dipping into it when necessary to keep him in expensive liquor and tobacco.

Shipman planned to use some of it to buy a new ship; bigger and better than all before her, with a strong and able crew. The rest he would take with him where he would sail the oceans living like a king in his cruising fortress with the seven seas as a moat.

Shipman held out his lantern as he climbed over the jagged rocks, which were covered in slimy seaweed making this a hazardous mission. Hopping from one rock to another and catching the occasional soaking wave, he continued towards the entrance to the cavern which was just discernible through the sea spray and darkening night.

A dark form lying on the rocks ahead forced Shipman to stop dead in his tracks. Peering through the sea spray he could see it was a body, a body of a man all big and swollen with seawater or worse. Clambering over to the body Shipman held his lantern up over the man's face and gasped. It was Captain Balthazar Blyberg. Shipman slipped on the slimy seaweed in his surprise and fell backwards but somehow managed to keep his lantern from smashing on the rocks. Now back on unsteady feet, Shipman re-examined Blyberg's body and bellowed in delight, for it wasn't the captain, not exactly. What Shipman's lantern revealed was the bulky figurehead effigy of Blyberg, carved by the captain's own hands so many years since. The figurehead somehow had broken free from the Gypsea and had been carried by the sea to finish up coincidentally at the same cove as Shipman. A reminder, thought the superstitious pirate; maybe sent by Blyberg's ghost who wanted him to know there was still a score to settle.

Shipman saw that his dagger was still embedded in the wood and a shredded piece of Blyberg's shirt was still attached. He tried to remove his dagger but it wouldn't budge. With one foot, Shipman pushed Blyberg's figurehead off the rocks, and waited for the splash it made as it returned to the sea, before he continued towards the cavern.

When Shipman reached the mouth of the cavern he paused briefly before entering. It was dark inside and the wind was playing tricks on him, distorting the sound of a hoard of roosting gulls high up on the cliff tops. He thought he heard a whispering voice calling to him from a lonely place far out to sea, cursing him. Shaking his head to remove any more foolish, fanciful thoughts he entered the cavern.

Shipman had climbed to the top of the pile of boulders at the far end of the cavern. Holding his lantern above his head, he saw the fissure that old Sam had described to him and prepared to heave himself up and into the upper chamber. He stopped what he was doing momentarily to listen to a new sound emanating from somewhere near the exit. It was a creaking sound, faint but growing steadily louder. It reminded Shipman of the sound of deck planks on a ship as they bowed and rasped under the strain of the changing weathers. Ignoring it, he heaved himself through to the upper chamber.

The large casket was carefully opened and he gasped at the sheer amount of treasures contained within.

"Crafty old sod!" he chuckled to himself as he fingered the pearly threads and sparkling gems. "Ouch!" All of a sudden Shipman yelped as he brushed a nasty looking black spider off his hand. The spider had bitten into him and blood began to ooze from a puncture wound in one of his veins. In the gloom, he listened to a swarming sound coming from all around. His lantern gave away its mystery.

The cavern walls and ceiling were a teeming mass of the same black mephitic creatures. The spiders could smell his blood and seemed to be attracted to his lantern's light.

"Jesus wept!" he gasped and he

dragged the casket over to the fissure in the floor. Securing the lid, Shipman pushed the casket through and followed it quickly to the lower chamber. Brushing off some residual spiders that were attached to him and had half buried themselves under his exposed skin, Shipman began to drag the casket behind him as he made his way towards the cavern exit. The passage out was clearly visible due to a full moon that reflected off the sea and caused a rippling effect along the walls and ceiling nearest the exit. Shipman stopped dragging the heavy casket; he needed to rest and he sat down to regain his breath. Free from the noise of the dragging casket he could again hear that same creaking sound and not only that, he was aware of the lurching shadow of a man slowly advancing down the tunnel towards him.

"So you wants to defend your treasure do you!" shouted Shipman thinking it was Sam. He had tied the old man to his rocking chair before leaving Gull Tower to find the casket. Sam was barely alive but any pirate will defend his loot, even to the death.

"This time I'll finish you off!" Shipman hollered and he picked up a fairsized rock and walked towards the creaking shadow. As he drew nearer to the lumbering shape he realised it was way too big to be Sam; in fact it was way too big to be a man of any normal kind. Shipman stood with mouth agape, as he felt more fear now than at any time during his many years of piracy. Ahead of him was the towering form of Captain Balthazar Blyberg's figurehead, somehow animate, somehow alive. With a dry rotten creak, it lumbered onwards.

Shipman overcame his paralysis and hurled the rock which bounced off Blyberg's facsimile without leaving a mark. He was only feet away from the figurehead when it spoke to him.

"I've come for you Shipman. You betrayed me and you betrayed the Gypsea. I told you I was immortal, I told you all, now I is back!" The figurehead sounded a little like Blyberg when it spoke but the words were masked by a gurgling, throaty, rasp that came from its chiselled deadpan features. Shipman noticed that when the figure spoke, a black, thick, miry slime oozed from its carved lips and dead eyes, and he found it difficult to believe this reality. Leaving the casket and lantern he dodged past the hulking wooden Blyberg and bolted out of the cavern as fast as his legs would carry him.

"You can't escape me, I'll find you wherever you are, split you open I will, I will, I wiiiiiiiiiiiiiiiiiiiiiiiiiiiiiiiiiiiiiiiiil!"

Climbing the slippery rocks, Shipman headed back towards Gull Tower. Like a moth attracted to a flame, he climbed the rocks as fast as he could until his hands bled. Stalked by the unrelenting creaking death below, its haunting taunts and cries only made Shipman climb faster and higher. At last he was on the cliff top. Exhausted, he fell onto his back and gulped in the night air before crawling to the edge to peer over the top and look down below. There was no creaking. No lumbering wooden figure could be seen. Shipman got to his feet and laughed loudly, a nervous laugh.

"Ha, I imagined it. Ye gods, I must be losing me brains. Too many years at sea," he squawked and he walked towards Sam's cottage.

7

Inside the cottage Shipman found Sam, slumped and bound to his chair right where he had left him. The bottle of rum was still on the table and he pulled out its cork and took an ample swig. *CREAAAAAK*, came a sound behind him. He whirled around but was confronted only with the open door to the cottage. The door swung slightly in the night's breeze; the hinges were rusty and the door creaked. Shipman placed a hand over his heart.

"Jesus wept!" he cried and walked over to bolt the door shut. He sat down at Sam's table and played with the coins contained in the small iron chest; he was stacking the coins and counting them.

"So you never found me casket then eh?" said Sam who was now awake and watching Shipman tot up the coin stacks.

"I found your casket all right, no doubt about that."

"Left it outside the cottage then have you?" enquired the old man.

"I left it in the cavern if you must know. I'll bring it up in the morning, now shut your maw or I'll shut it for you!" spat an angered Shipman. He was angry at himself for being afraid. Afraid to go back down to the cavern to collect Sam's treasure. Afraid he might imagine something. Something big, something horrible, lurking in the shadows down there.

Sam, although awake, didn't look too

good. His head was swollen now from the assault with the heavy key. He was still spitting loose teeth and clotted blood. In order to gain some comfort, he rocked in his chair, but the creaking wood agitated Shipman who warned Sam to stop. Shipman was finding it hard to keep awake. He had almost finished the last of the rum and his bristly chin was slumped onto his chest as he sat at the table.

"Will you stop that bloody noise," he shouted. "I won't tell you again." Shipman threw an angry glance over at Sam, but the old man was motionless in his chair, and the creaking continued.

Shipman sprung to his feet. The creaking sound was coming from outside the cottage. Racing over to the bolted door he put an ear to it. The creaking was getting louder as something drew nearer the cottage.

"What you doing lad?" asked Sam bewildered by Shipman's behaviour.

"Can you not hear it?" responded

Shipman as he moved back from the door. There followed a series of strident thumping on the cottage door, so forceful that the bolt began to bend and the door planks began to crack and splinter.

"It be him, he's come for me! Jesus he's come for me!" wailed the now terrified Shipman.

"Who's come for you lad? What be banging on me door?" Sam's words were silenced by the shattering of the cottage door that fell into the room in a heap of splintered sticks. Stepping through the broken doorframe came Blyberg's figurehead.

"*Shhhhipman.* I wants you, I wants you dead Shipman, an I'll have you dead!" gurgled the monstrous shape. The figurehead plucked out Shipman's dagger from its chest and closed its chiselled mitts around the hilt.

"Splits you open I will. *Ssssplitssss* you open and feed you to the gulls," it groaned oozing its ghastly sludge. Shipman raced through the heavy door that joined the cottage to the lighthouse. He slammed the door shut but couldn't lock it. The ring of keys was on the table with Sam. His heart was pounding and he felt dizzy with fear. Too scared to move and too scared not to, Shipman began to climb the black iron spiral staircase to the top of Gull Tower.

"Heavens to Betsy! Would you look at that," exclaimed Sam as Blyberg's figurehead clumped along the floor towards him. Struggling with his bonds, Sam made a useless effort to escape and finally gave in to his fate. The figurehead raised its weapon.

"I takes no *prisonerssss*," gurgled the ligneous terror, and it plunged its dagger into the helpless chest of Sam. With jerky precision Sam was filleted.

Shipman was half way up the staircase when he heard the first footfall of Blyberg's figurehead. The heavy wood and iron made a resonating sound that together with the devil's loathsome cackling almost caused him to faint on the spot.

"I am coming for you *Sssshipman*."

Finally, at the top of the tower, Shipman closed the heavy iron door. This time there was a latch and he slid it across. This door may stop it he thought, and it better, for there was no place left to run. One hundred and forty feet up and under the stars, Shipman circled the burning beacon feverishly searching for a weapon. All the time he searched, the sound of the figurehead's clumping feet on the iron staircase could be heard, growing louder as it reached the top of the tower.

At last the clumping stopped and was replaced with a loud banging as the figurehead pummelled its fists on the iron door. Shipman could do nothing except pray, to whatever gods listened to the prayers of pirates, that the door would hold. Great dents appeared in the door that must have been at the very least three inches thick. Shipman held his breath and pressed himself hard against the tower rail. A dagger's blade, making Shipman jump almost out of his skin, then punctured the door. The blade began to cut a hole in the iron as though the door itself was made of cheese.

"No...no!" yelped Shipman as the square plug of iron fell out of the door and clanged onto the floor. Stepping through the hole came the figurehead, dagger raised, slime oozing from its perpetually grinning face.

"Now I have you, you can't *essscape* me now," the figurehead gurgled and lumbered over to Shipman.

"Get away from me, you're dead. Dead I tells you!" Shipman screeched as the towering monster closed in for the kill.

"*Splitsss* you open I will," it said menacingly. Shipman let go of the rail and ignoring his fear he charged at the figurehead and somehow managed to knock it off balance. The figurehead fell backwards and smashed into the glass chimney that housed the burning wick of the beacon. First the arm of the figurehead caught fire, but it only took seconds for the hungry flames to engulf its whole being. Still it came, a roaring ball of flames lurching towards Shipman.

"Fire can't stop me, nor can the sea, I will carry out my curse on you," yelled the ball of fire as it collided with the petrified Shipman.

Stealing the brightness from Gull Tower, the burning figurehead and Shipman toppled over the rail and fell a long way down to the unforgiving rocks below. To Shipman the journey down seemed to be horribly suspended. The force of the air swept back the flames on the figurehead's charred face producing a mane of burning locks. The one thing he would remember on his fall was the malodorous stench that emanated from the burning horror that gripped him so tightly. Sparks soared aloft into the darkness as the entwined pair hit the rocks below.

8

Shipman was in a land of dreams, a land of nightmares. He dreamt he was being dragged over stone and that the sharp glass like rocks were cutting his flesh like knives. Another dream found him trapped inside the treasure casket like a cramped coffin, unable to move his arms or legs, with Blyberg standing over him casting shovels of sand and dirt into the casket. He was being buried alive.

Shipman woke from his dreaming but

found himself in a worse nightmare. He was awake, but he couldn't see. There was nothing but a darkened veil of blackness. Worse still he was racked in excruciating pain and he could not move. He had broken his back in the fall as well as practically every other bone in his body. It was a miracle he was alive, but in his paralysed state he wished he wasn't. Shipman yelled out in pain until his throat was hoarse but fell silent after becoming aware of an odour. The faint stench of smouldering wood wafted over him. Moving only his eyes, because that was all he could move, he could see something to his right. As his eyes became adjusted to the darkness, a few pockets of smouldering orange embers began to move towards him and they creaked.

Light formed around Shipman as he lay on a hard, cold, stone floor. A lantern lit by a glowing finger stump of Blyberg's figurehead gave away their location, and he could see he was back in the upper chamber of the cavern. To his left he could just about make out the casket of treasure. To his right stood the charred smouldering remains of Blyberg's figurehead. The figurehead was badly damaged from its fire and fall; missing one arm and the top of its head. The smoking hulk spoke.

"*Ssstill* I live Shipman, I live to see you die!" Shipman became aware of a surge of movement as the walls and ceiling of the cavern seemed to flow towards him, towards the lantern. In minutes, the first of the spiders began to bite. Unable to move Shipman screamed in agony as he was slowly eaten alive under the watchful, lank, emotionless mask of Blyberg's figurehead.

"Eaten by the crabs I was. Now *it'sss* your turn to die!" The echoing, chilling laughter of Blyberg's spirit filled the upper chamber and drifted out and upwards to join the chirps and calls of the roosting gulls and the moaning wind that etched its presence into the cliffs of

Gull Cove.

The Lady o' the night stood dark and deserted for many a month until the day old Sam Finn's body was found, but nobody found Shipman's body for many a decade. When they did, all they found was a clean picked skeleton of broken bones; no trace of a casket containing treasure, and no trace of a curiously burned and damaged ship figurehead. Maybe the treasure was taken from the cavern by others fortuitous enough to find it. Maybe the creaking spirit of Captain Balthazar Blyberg dragged it away and out to sea to where his body lay in the murky depths, amongst the seaweed, and the barnacle encrusted wreck of the vessel Gypsea.

The author would appreciate an Amazon and Goodreads review.

I do read all the reviews each and every one and I am very grateful to anyone who has taken the time to post a review. I appreciate the time you have taken reading this story. I hope you enjoyed reading it as much as I enjoyed writing it.

You are welcome to join David on his Facebook page and group where you can receive news about forthcoming releases, and also to discuss and share thoughts and queries about any of David's published works.

https://www.facebook.com/davidralphwilliams

For more information on the complete range of David Ralph Williams' fiction visit Amazon's author page or David's website:

https://davidralphwilliams.webs.com

Printed in Dunstable, United Kingdom